The Tale of a Stupid Boy

Stories of a kid growing up in an Australian country town

Some of these stories may actually be true

Written and Illustrated By

M. J. Stewart

 A catalogue record for this book is available from the National Library of Australia

This book is, of course, fiction.

Publisher:
Australian Self Publishing Group, Pty. Ltd / Inspiring Publishers
PO Box 159, Calwell, ACT 2905, Australia.
Phone: 61-(0) 2 6291-2904
http://australianselfpublishinggroup.com

National Library of Australia Prepublication Data Service

Author: M. J. Stewart

Title: **The Tale of a Stupid Boy**

ISBN: 978-1-923449-84-8 (print)
ISBN: 978-1-923250-45-1 (ePub2)

This book is dedicated to every single
'Stupid Boy'
I've known in my life.

You know who you are.

✧

Prologue

'If You Believe This ....'

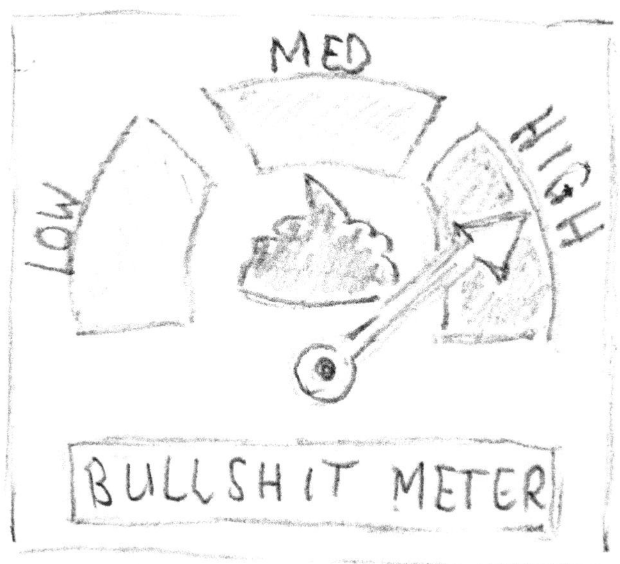

Born into a half-British half-Asian family in the eastern suburb of Welshpool, north-east of Perth, Western Australia, I was obviously too much of a distraction for the family after birth.

Mum and Dad already had seven children and felt the added financial stress coupled with the lack of room and living space in our home was just too much to reasonably bear. The family was obviously quite large, and being of limited means, I was placed with an adoption agency at a young age - what was I to do?

As traumatic as I'm sure this whole episode was for the family, I still struggle to understand the actual mechanics of the adoption process. I can, however, remember the looks of anguish on the faces of my parents as they grappled with this *life-altering* decision. I do realise it was the best option for all involved but still, an incredibly difficult part of my formative years.

I have been told that our house in Western Australia was small, but pretty, painted white with a white picket fence and had a lovely little rose garden in the front yard. Apparently, a nice house in a lovely part of the country.

I particularly still miss my biological grandfather *Wan Hung Low*. He taught me so much. An accomplished chef and a caring person who *doted* on me during my wonderful (although brief) time in Western Australia. I especially loved his *secret* fried rice recipe which he meticulously taught me over many months and which I do still cook to this day: DELICIOUS.

My four brothers Yo-Ling Ping; We-In Chow; Sun-Su and Sam, and my three sisters Mary; Libby and Xian Jong were saddened for many years after I left and to this day are still traumatised by the upheaval to the family. My departure was obviously *gut-wrenching* to all involved but, as they say, *such is life*.

In the ensuing years we tried to stay in touch with each other, but it was obviously difficult, mainly because I had been adopted out to a family on the east coast and so the huge distance needed to travel from the west coast of Australia was daunting to say the least. It eventually became too hard and distressing, so everyone needed to just *move on*. In the end, it was also emotionally difficult for me to *go back* through that part of my life whilst trying to deal with the normal *rigours* of my new life. Early childhood, preschool, primary school and ultimately high school became a moving *blur*, once I'd been adopted to a beautiful family just north of Newcastle, New South Wales.

Although limited, I did enjoy some contact with many of the members of my biological family. Improvements in technology and cheaper access to airline travel was so comforting and such a relief given the sadness and confusion that would have been caused by *'.... just not knowing where I came from...'* (I guess).

With my new family though, I found two new sisters (at that time) who eventually became three new sisters and one new brother plus a loving mother and a genuinely involved father. I officially became a STEWART.

For the sake of protecting everyone's privacy I will call my *new-found* Mum JOY and my *new-found* Dad MARSHALL. Maybe my *new-found* *overprotective* siblings could be called JUDITH, DIANE, RAYMOND and MURIEL for the sake of this exercise. I'm sure they will know who they are after reading a few of these stories anyway.

We don't need any unnecessary litigation by revealing anyone's real identity, do we?

Chapter One
Introduction

'A Growing Family on the Move'

(Quote: ME)

Well, if you're still reading this you may need to take a breather. I must provide a little bit of *context* to my family upbringing so you can understand which parts of this story are *real* and which parts, *aren't*.

Firstly, everything I've written about my adoption and being born in Western Australia is a big *fat* lie. This concept of my early *life* described above always tickled my fancy as a sad, involved, tragic story about a young cub who had been let go by his loving family due to circumstances beyond his limited control. Just pathetic really.

Although, in fairness to me, most of my STEWART siblings believed this story after I described it to them over many years. They genuinely wanted me to have been adopted, I guess, because I was so different to them. Happy and healthy but just a little bit awkward.

It should be noted, too, that quite a few of the following stories are *made up* or *fabrications* of an *active imagination*. My wonderful imagination is something I tried very hard to harness whilst growing up in my formative years. You may also like to know that some other stories are *partially* true but embellished (a lot) with lies.

Anyway, read on, enjoy, and see if you can pick out the real stories.

In the real world, I was born to beautiful parents (Joy and Marshall) in a popular housing commission area in the small township of Raymond Terrace (just north of Newcastle in New South Wales). Like most families in the 1960's, we had limited means but managed a strong will to grow and move forward through whatever vagaries life decided to throw our way.

I had two older sisters at this stage and Dad had a good solid job as a plumber working in support trades services at the RAAF Base at Williamtown. Mum cooked, cleaned, could sew and make clothes, and was looking forward to making the family grow a little more by having more children.

By way of explanation, Dad was a champion bloke, well liked by his friends and work colleagues and held in high regard by Mum's family. He was a hard worker, funny and loved Mum and "us" kids above all else. It must have been hard for him, though, living so far away from his family in Far North Queensland, although he never complained. He did have high standards where his work around the house and property was concerned, so it was difficult to help him as we grew older, as he preferred to "… do it once and do it right …" rather than watch us stuff it up, lose his temper, and then redo it himself anyway. He loved a beer, smoked cigarettes back in the day and was always working.

Mum, too, was very popular throughout the community, as she was always helpful, engaging and a willing participant if things needed to be done. Mum loved to keep the "peace", enforced punishment under sufferance, and was recognised as a good worker. Great sense of humour but very naïve, particularly where conversations turned to "smutty" jokes, sex or relationships. She never drank alcohol or swore and was widely appreciated by her family and friends. At times, Mum did appreciate to be left alone to rest and read books, although these opportunities didn't present very often.

By the time I reached the ripe old age of six months Dad and Mum had purchased a property at Medowie (on *Hire Purchase* at incredibly high interest rates we learnt later in life). An incredibly expensive way to purchase property but the will to own our own home was strong.

The accommodation was *limited* and consisted of a two-bedroom corrugated iron shed on three acres. It did present as a great opportunity for a growing family with no money, heads full of dreams and a group of highly talented children. Wait a minute, that was the bloody *Von Trapp family* out of the *Sound of Music* - not us. We did have no money and heads full of dreams however, so two out of three 'ain't bad as they say in the classics.

Anyway, my younger brother Raymond and sister Muriel arrived in 1961 and Dad added a couple of rooms and worked harder, while Mum relied on support and help from the beautiful members of the Medowie community. Her amazing sewing and cooking skills were used to *barter* for fruit, vegetables, milk, eggs, and chickens. This proved to be an easy concept to understand when you appreciate the variety of *skills* possessed by the families in town.

As the kids grew older, we were lucky to be able to attend the local primary school a few kilometres from our home. Mum was able to get employment at the RAAF Base at Williamtown and the family that had nothing but love, moved on to the next part of their journey through life. Wonderful times growing up in the amazing community of Medowie.

Chapter Two

Medowie The Amazing 'Melting Pot'

'*A Real-Life Example of the Best Aspects of Immigration*'

(Quote: ME)

Our new home was nestled in a small village approximately 35 kilometres from Newcastle and a similar distance from Maitland (considered the gateway to the renowned grape-growing region of the Hunter Valley) in New South Wales.

Predominantly rural, with many fruit orchards and farms, a primary school, two small businesses and an amazing mix of culturally diverse and racially varied families from many countries around the globe.

I always wondered if the *influx* of immigrants following WWII was specifically *planned* by the Government of the day or if it just a brilliant co-incidence. I'll never know, I guess.

So many beautiful families like the Boshevs, Dykmans, Winkelmans, Van Kerkhoffs, Boyds; Tarasins Stokess, Luxtons, Ramels, Muirs, Galloways, Coxs, Pierces, Bickfords, Moxeys; Tickles; Barracks; Stewarts; Sneddons; Szabunias, Cappiellos, Kaweckyjs, Sneddons Peggs, Tams, Komoroskis, Jones, Sharps, Osborns, Wests, Wilkinsons, Georgious, Stefinaks, Kacubas, Murfins, Bartons and just so many more. What a treat to be able to be a small part of the lives of so many families, in one small town, from so many cultural backgrounds. Very lucky indeed.

Not many kids can say they've been kicked up the arse by so many people, from so many nationalities, just for being a dickhead. I felt like a very lucky *Stupid Boy.*

To witness a community bond and work together for the betterment of everyone's lives was truly great. A concept from which everyone benefitted. Some cooked, some sewed, some farmed, some helped break down language barriers, some helped at the school. Goods and clothing were *passed down* to younger kids once no longer needed and not one family seemed to have the faintest idea about racism or prejudice. As kids we certainly didn't. In fact, I can't recall witnessing any such behaviours growing up. I did, however, see some other things that *beggared* belief as you will notice in the following collection of stories.

The place was always *buzzing* on weekends due to the large influx of cars and people looking to purchase fruit and vegetables from the many roadside stalls. These offered the local farmers a chance to pick up some extra cash from tourists without too much effort. The stalls looked after themselves, or were manned by the children, and gave the farmer an opportunity to get most of his produce ready for the regional markets on Monday mornings.

The town gained a very distinct *identity* throughout the lower Hunter Valley for its fine produce and particularly the *highly sought-after* stone fruits like peaches, plums, and nectarines. Other produce such as strawberries, mixed vegetables and eggs also featured.

It also gave other locals, such as Mum and Dad, an opportunity to collect some cheaper produce without leaving the district. This not only helped the weekly budget, I must say, but it also supported the farmers, producers and growers, and their families.

At various stages, Dad also tried his hand at growing vegetables (quite successfully although somewhat labour intensive). We happily sold the produce along the roadside at the front of our property on weekends for him: for a fee, of course.

Chapter Three
Back to My Real Birth

'The Most Important Day of My Life'
(Quote: ME)

It's obviously an amazing thing when children enter this world and join the cast of *family life*. To witness a young couple enjoying the pure wonderment and unbridled joy of the birth of their own child is amazing. Dare I say, truly one of nature's marvels.

Mum and Dad were married in 1955 and moved to Innisfail in Far North Queensland soon thereafter. This was Dad's place of birth and his original *hometown*, so they were surrounded by a large, wonderful family and So many familiar places and faces from dad's childhood.

In 1956 my sister Jude was born at Innisfail Base Hospital and life for the newly-weds was pretty good. The only problem was that Mum struggled with the heat and humidity in Far North Queensland and inevitably the young family needed to relocate to a *cooler climate*. Newcastle seemed a logical choice: Mum's parents lived in Stockton and Mum grew up, attended school, and worked in the suburbs surrounding. Her sisters and brother also lived there in the early days, which gave Mum some much-needed comfort and support.

An opportunity arose in Raymond Terrace for housing and Dad managed an employment opportunity as an apprentice plumber in the support services at RAAF Base Williamtown. A good outcome all round for the growing family.

Now Jude could best be described as the "leader" of her siblings and enjoyed a great sense of humour. She was very strong-willed, like Dad, and called us out when we stuffed up or "... went too far ..." Jude owned up, when necessary (not often), was very practical and gave us a wide berth if anything we did looked like getting out of control or could implicate her.

My sister Diane was born at The Mater Hospital, Newcastle in 1957 and so the little family started to grow. Life was apparently good, and everyone was happy.

Diane was more reserved than Jude, a bit more like Mum than Dad, and very diplomatic. She looked to avoid conflict wherever possible and was a good thinker, to the point that she was often lost in her own thoughts rather than "making mayhem" like some of her siblings.

Mum fell pregnant again in 1959 and so the family was ready to grow again. Help was provided by Mums sisters & mother as they rallied around to support in whatever way possible - an expectant Mum with two toddlers could not have been easy. Dad was working hard with a good job, so they dreamed of ultimately buying a home of their own.

For the moment though they concentrated on the *day-to-day* struggle, unaware of a bit of *rough* weather on the horizon.

As the date drew closer for the birth of their third child, Mum was feeling unwell and, whilst coping alright, became a little worried about the health of the unborn child. Doctors too believed Mums pulse had become erratic; her health wasn't the best and her *well-being* became a bit of a concern.

As the day drew near Mum was admitted to The Mater Hospital and Dad relied on Nan and Pop and Mums sisters for some help and support. He needed to work but was happy knowing the girls were being cared for and were safe. He visited Mum after work for support & hoped all would be well with Mum and the new *Bub*.

On a Saturday morning in January 1960, he visited early, and the Doctors spoke to him about the impending birth. Things were looking a bit grim as they struggled to find a pulse for the unborn child. Dad still waited, all the while hoping for the best, and left the doctors to go about the job of running a very busy hospital.

By mid-afternoon the doctors' confidence was waning, and they suggested he should probably go home: they believed there was little hope for a 'live' birth. Dad left the hospital as suggested after ensuring Mum was comfortable, and as well as could be expected. He drove to Nan and Pop's house in Stockton and walked down to The Gladstone Hotel where Nan worked, feely somewhat helpless, I'm sure.

After a couple of hours and a few schooners of beer, Dad waited for some news. The hospital finally called Nan at the Pub in the early evening to tell them Mum had given birth to a healthy (6 pounds 10 ounces) bouncing baby boy – ME. The drama surrounding the birth had more to do with Mums deep veins and the inability of the medical staff to find a strong pulse (apparently), rather than a serious issue with the baby, as the story goes.

Mum came home in about a week with me wrapped up like a bundle of joy. The whole disaster was averted and no one's life in our family would ever be the same.

Chapter Four

Rounding Out the Family

'In Fall the Final Pieces of the Jigsaw Puzzle'
(Quote: ME)

Shortly thereafter Mum fell pregnant again with an expectation that she would be giving birth around September or October 1961. Already a handful, her three kids made family life more like a whirlwind rather than idyllic. Dad, whilst working as hard as he could, was a great comfort for Mum but the enormous help from her mother and sisters scattered around the Newcastle area was invaluable. They played a role in helping Mum stay sane and manage to have (an almost) *event-free* pregnancy.

October 1961 arrived, and Mum was whisked into hospital (a familiar road by now) and gave birth to …. TWINS. Bloody hell, that wasn't in the script. Raymond arrived first and then an hour & half later Muriel came out for a look around. Mum and Dad were now the *chuffed* and proud parents of five kids all under the age of five.

The downside, of course, was that everything was now multiplied, and life became both more costly and a little more difficult to handle. Small issues became big issues. One kid gets measles, a cold, the 'flu or any other bug and you can multiply that by five immediately. One kid needs shoes so generally do the other four and so on and so forth.

Raymond was a real "straight-shooter" and easily disappointed (mostly by me and the outcome of some of my brilliant ideas). He rarely strayed far and generally towed the line, which kept potential floggings to a minimum. Ray hated being "roped into" things because he was smart enough to see that often the outcome involved pain or trouble, or both. Great sense of humour though and took much joy from watching me get whacked.

Muriel was more the quiet and reserved type, but she also hated Being "roped into" things given the outcomes were usually predictable, at best. She felt some pressure from being the youngest of the family, so whilst happy to engage with her siblings, rather than being left out, she also could see danger lurking, resulting from some of the idiotic games suggested by me. Muriel too had a good sense of humour but did often feel others pain when they were in trouble and being handed the usual forms of punishment.

The question often asked about Ray and Muriel: were they exactly alike being twins? No. In fact, in some ways, they were more like chalk and cheese than twins. In no way, however, did that impact on their "day-to-day" lives. They just laughed and loved growing up in Medowie.

Just after the twins were born, Mum and Dad decided to drive from Newcastle to Innisfail in Far North Queensland in a station wagon with five kids under five years of age. Not a good idea I'm afraid. The enormous floods across NSW and QLD that year were manageable but five kids screaming and vomiting from *chicken pox*, or generally just five kids arguing most of the way must have tested anyone's sanity. Certainly not an ideal situation for anyone.

Dad's family, and our relatives, were obviously overjoyed to catch up with us and genuinely appreciated meeting the newborn kids for the first time, but what an ordeal.

We survived that trip but, strangely enough, we caught the train next time.

Chapter Five
Medowie Primary School

'Little School – Big Hearts'

(Quote: ME)

'm guessing not many kids remember much about their early days at school, but I have a couple of recollections that may be of interest.

Finally, a chance to send me off to school and give Mum a break from my constant wanderings to the neighbours' houses begging for food, to the *never-ending* requests for someone to peel snails for me so I could eat them. Weird, I know. For some reason I loved eating garden snails, and often could be found sitting on the ground with copious amounts of snail slime across my face after devouring (who knows) how many of the little morsels. Nan always enjoyed entertaining me so she could often be found just peeling the shells off them for me, knowing how much I loved them. You *'gotta* love Nan.

So, it was about time for me to go to school at the tender age of four.

Mum walked me into the office on Day 1 and introduced me to the Principal, Mr Earp. I was shuffled off to meet my Kindergarten teacher: Mrs Forrest, who diligently watched and nurtured her flock of children with patience and style. From the little blowup *pillows*, we slept on after lunchtime, to the myriad of stencils we coloured and hung around the room before Christmas, my classroom memories are of genuine joy and happiness.

One recollection revolved around the use of the little *chalkboards* attached to the back wall and used for drawing pictures and learning numbers. Strangely my mind always takes me to the afternoon one of the girls (her name was Gai), was standing using these boards and just decided to 'pee' on the floor. She didn't really move, and no one really knew what to do except watch. Don't know why I remember this story, but I always have. It is one of many memories from the earlier days of primary school.

Another similar recollection evolved a couple of years later and it begins in the same classroom, although the event itself was a little more *sophisticated.*

By Second Class we had been taught to raise our hand to ask permission when we wanted to go the toilets. One of the young fellas called Andrew had his hand up to go but Mrs Forrest was writing on the board and had her back turned to the class. Things became urgent as the young lad yelled out his intentions to run to the 'loo and the teacher said '*...quick then, run...*'. We all watched as he tried to cover the 100 metres to the back of the playground where the toilets were located. Sadly, he had shit running down the back of his legs at the 50metre mark. Embarrassing for Andrew, obviously, but great theatre for the rest of the class.

I think Andrew and his brother left the school shortly thereafter but I'm not sure why?

It does seem that young kids have an amazing fascination with *wee and poo* stories. I was no different, I guess.

One final thing that fascinated me about "little school" was the number of kids that ate the "paste" we used to stick posters into books, or notes onto cardboard. I'm sure it was harmless and probably tasted great, but the "old Perkins Paste" was a big favourite of the pupils. Obviously, I have to be a little careful here though, because I ate garden snails regularly, so people in "glass houses", as they say. Maybe paste would have been more appetising?

Chapter Six
School Canteen

'Every Kids Deserves a Good Feed'

(Quote: ME)

Who could forget school canteen. We were lucky enough to have the local mums throw together a *Tuck Shop* for the kids once a month on a Monday at lunchtime. This included *home-made* chicken soup, sandwiches, cakes and biscuits, Nicholsons' pies and sausage rolls (which were delivered), fruit from the local farmers, small bottles of soft drink and flavoured milk. Amazingly you could buy a large pie, soft drink and a cake for 20cents: bargain even back in the day.

Everyone was excited when they knew the *Tuck Shop* would be in operation the following week: it just added another dimension to the experience of primary school. To some degree, the teachers were as happy about it as the pupils.

It demonstrates yet again the wonderful ability to get together and create something for the good of the children in a small community in country Australia. Everyone who was able helped, either by cooking, serving, cleaning, delivering or just ensuring their own children availed themselves of the foods on offer.

The kids felt like they belonged to a community and some much-needed funds were raised for the school. Certainly, a *win-win* for everyone involved.

I always suspected this was a good opportunity to ensure that all the kids were fed, irrespective of their financial situation, such was the quality of the beautiful people who resided in this town. Certainly, items such as school uniforms, other clothes, shoes, jumpers and sporting gear were regularly *passed around* between families to both ensure their continued use and that no children looked *out of place* when it came to school or sport.

Just wonderful country families growing up in a small country town.

The *Tuck Shop* concept was certainly a winner for the kids. So too was the government initiative of providing small bottles of fresh milk daily for primary school children around Australia back in the 1960s and 1970s. Sadly this was *phased out* a long time ago, although it does make you wonder why?

Chapter Seven

My First Kiss

'That Girl Has a Lovely Personality'

(Quote: MUM)

As we moved into First Class (same classroom and same teacher but a step up the ladder on our way to university), we were assigned different seats after kindergarten the previous year. I was lucky enough to be seated next to Narelle which was great. She seemed a nice person and (of course) Mum and Dad knew her Mum and Dad very well, and they were good friends.

Anyway, I was enjoying the experience and looking forward to finding new friends, which I imagined was what school was all about. Each of the school days were moving along nicely, and we genuinely became embroiled in new fun things to keep us all busy. That was UNTIL the day Narelle shoved her head *right in* next to my face … and … kissed me. Boy, that was a new experience for a kid six years of age.

I understood when the cousins, aunts, uncles, and grandparents turned up you had to spend an hour kissing them hello and then again before they all went home. That was generally considered to be normal behaviour, apparently. You didn't even kiss your sisters to be honest.

So, I did what every young male would probably do under the circumstances: I "over-reacted" a little bit. I screamed, jumped out of my seat, started waving my arms all over the place and, basically, carried on like a *dick*. The teacher thought I was having a *fit*. Far more aggressive than required under the circumstances, I believe. The result wasn't any punishment for poor Narelle, but in me being made to stand in the corner of the room (facing the wall) for the rest of the lesson. Oh, the shame of it all.

Who knew that a kiss was, really, *acceptable behaviour.* What an absolute *Stupid Boy.*

Obviously, Mum and Dad got word of this episode and I was dealt with *appropriately* (just to satisfy Narelle's parents I think, not because I behaved like a knob).

✦

Chapter Eight

School Bee Hives

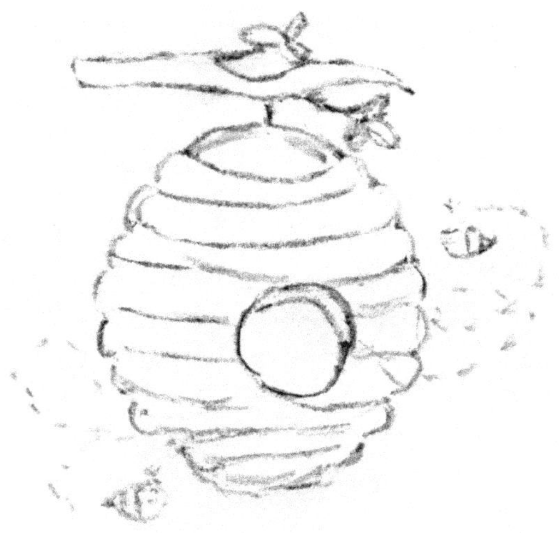

Imagine being both allergic to, and absolutely petrified of, insects. Specifically in this case, bees. An awful predicament I can only imagine. As kids in primary school, we obviously lacked understanding, empathy, and compassion to Almost every aspect of life, so our reaction to finding one of the kids in school had such allergies was not only *mind-boggling*, but it presented us with a unique opportunity (or so we thought).

This pupil was one of the kids in fourth class, and he suffered from a severe allergy to bees. In our tiny little minds, we thought (maybe) we could help him out, or (maybe) even cure him of such an affliction. So, a few of us from fifth and sixth class decided it would be a good idea to carry him down to the *School Bee Hives* near the monkey bars and sandpits, adjacent to the boundary fence adjoining Boshevs' farm, just to see what would happen. We were convinced we could help him in the way that only a "caring" ten-year-old or an eleven-year-old kid could help a fellow student.

He squirmed and screamed a lot while we were carrying him, which was interesting, to say the least. As we thought we were helping, however, we persevered almost to the point of exhaustion. It became apparent after a long while that we were ABSOLUTELY NOT helping the poor kid, we were just *pissing* him off. Certainly not our intended aim, I believe.

Fortunately for all concerned, the young fella managed to escape on his own and was luckily not stung by the bees, so a potential disaster was averted. In hindsight, totally idiotic behaviour for all concerned. I mean, what kid, who was highly allergic to something that could kill him, would appreciate being exposed to danger by a large group of "idiots". Another tick in the box for *Stupid Boy* and his wonderfully original ideas.

To this day, I can't seem to work out how this idea was ever considered a good one, except that kids can be many things growing up, including *cruel.*

Chapter Nine
Sticks up Skirts

'You Can't Put Brains in a Brick'
(Quote: DAD)

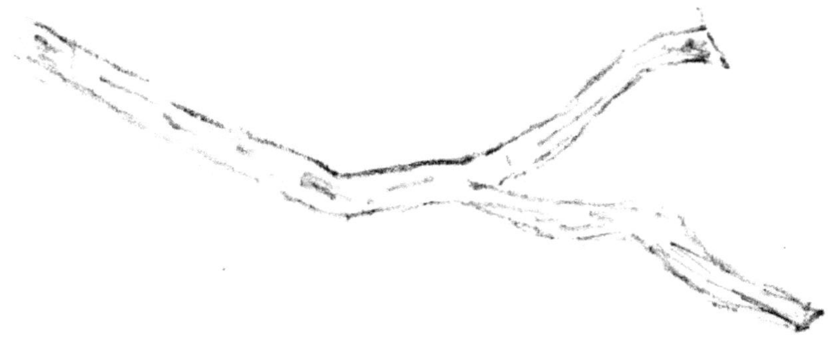

Kids love games and adventures and running around the playground At recess and lunchtime. In fact, this part of the school day was super special. In a small school of sixty-one students (from kindergarten to sixth class) you had to invent a few *games* which suited such a range of ages and athletic abilities. We had to pass the *limited* time spent out of class somehow.

There were a few favourites: like getting a silver aluminium milk bottle top, placing a ten-cent coin underneath and stamping on it with the heel of your shoe on the concrete. The resulting *image* on the bottle top looked exactly like a ten-cent coin when partially covered by sand and left lying on the ground in the playground. Just brilliant when you could hide behind a tree and watch some kids trying to pick it up thinking it was real money – very funny I thought.

Other standard games like cricket and soccer filled in a bit of time but generally needed an umpire or referee which was difficult to find when you only had a teaching pool of three.

One of the more sensible games we invented was called *Sticks Up Girls Dresses* which was a lot of fun but VERY unpopular with the teachers (only three teachers as mentioned, but unpopular just the same). It involved the girls standing on one side of the playground and the boys standing on the other side of the playground holding sticks. These sticks were found lying around the playground from the many trees in the school grounds.

The game would then start with a yell, and everyone would run towards each other as fast as they could. The aim was for the boys to try to use their stick to flick up the girls' skirts. What a huge load of fun for all concerned. Or so we thought, anyway.

The game was banned immediately and, amazingly, deemed *a stupid game.*

Seemed like a bit of harmless fun to us at the time.

Chapter Ten
School Fete and Pet Competition

'It's Not Always About Winning You Know'
(Quote: DAD)

The Primary School Fete was the day the kids were exposed to the craft; cooking and sewing skills of the local parents. Goods and homewares were exposed for sale to the students and their families, and everyone was encouraged to roam the school grounds, purchase jams; pickles; paintings; cakes; clothes and other goodies with proceeds from these sales going to the school.

Classrooms were thrown open for inspection by parents and visitors. The pupils' works were on display, and it gave parents a chance to catch up and chat in a relaxed environment.

The highlight for me, however, was the *Big Annual Pet Show*. Serious stuff for the enthusiastic kids who dreamed of an opportunity to have their pet *friends* judged and awarded prizes in a glittering awards ceremony at Medowie Primary. Not quite *glittering* perhaps but a highly anticipated amateur pet show none-the-less.

I immediately wondered what sort of pet I needed that could ultimately lead to a prize: chameleon, great white shark, penguin, giraffe, monkey or even a wombat? I finally settled on a pet which we actually had at home: a COW.

Who could resist a placid, *well-groomed* Friesian cow I thought, and it just so happened that we had a young heifer at home that fitted this description. I completed the application form and duly entered the competition in time to make the necessary arrangements for the big day: *The Medowie Primary School Big Annual Pet Show.*

I spent a few days washing, brushing, cleaning, and polishing *Freda the Friesian* for her inaugural day in the spotlight. It was a big job and by the morning of the show I felt I could do no more: the prize would surely be ours.

We lived about two kilometres from school, so my only option was to walk Freda early and get her settled in the playground ready for the show. I obviously didn't think through the logistics of this exercise, but I was only a kid. I threw a rope around her neck and off we walked to school: me and my 200kilogram pet. Even though it wasn't THAT far, it took hours to walk a cow to school: who knew?

As the day dragged on and the judging of the *Best Pet in Show* grew closer, I became more and more nervous - such a huge effort just to get Freda to the school let alone *imagine* winning the coveted award. The time drew near, and the crowd swelled around the *weather shed* in the middle of the playground where the judging was to be finalised.

Really nervous now as the head judge asked for quiet .... and the winner of the big Pet Show was .... *Barry the Budgerigar* owned by some *snotty-nosed* kindergarten kid whose name has always escaped me. I was gutted.

Second and third prizes raced by without even a mention of Freda and then, finally, the judges ended the show by handing out *Participation Certificates* to those of us who won *diddly squat*. I spent days washing, drying and brushing my pet then walking three hours to and from school with a 200kilogram cow for (basically) NOTHING. It was about this time in my life I started to understand what the term *Stupid Boy* really meant.

I would agree however that (perhaps) my *Pet Show* intentions weren't *pure* because I really wanted to win, and yes, this is just pathetic, I know.

Chapter Eleven
Family Life in Medowie

'Country Kids Always Have the Best Fun'
(Quote: ME)

Growing up in a small country town surrounded by the Australian bush sure was fun: particularly when you remember so many things you did that could have (or should have) resulted in serious injury or even death. Geez it was fun.

My two elder sisters still laugh at the time they locked me in a wardrobe when I was three years old and tried to set fire to it, hoping I would burn to death. Just hours of entertainment for all.

Around the same time my sisters also decided to run away from home. They packed a small suitcase with a teddy bear each, a Vegemite sandwich (from memory) and then ran down our driveway and up the road to find *freedom*. I ran after them crying because I didn't want them to go (yep - odd behaviour I know) and I was *almost* run over by a truck (so the story goes). Yet again just endless family fun when you live in the country.

We used to play in the yard for hours, days and weeks on-end and on reflection it was a wonderfully fun upbringing. We lived on one and a half hectares surrounded by fruit orchards and opposite *Muir's General Store* and chicken farm. We had a small chicken shed of our own, some fencing, a few fruit trees and a long driveway with a small house located about 100 metres from the main road. Occasionally we tried our hand at growing vegetables, raising a cow and some chickens, and making stewed and bottled fruit. A simple but good life.

There were weekend games of cricket at the oval or tennis at the adjacent courts. After a while however, the practice games of cricket had to be banned in Muir's front yard after too many kids were hit in the head with the cricket ball (significantly encouraged by the onlookers and met with howls of laughter every time someone was hit and went down). The number of panes of glass in the front windows replaced was also a factor, given the pitch was located only 30 metres from the front of the house and again, batsmen were encouraged to hit the ball as high and as hard as they could.

The Medowie area was surrounded by thousands of acres of the Australian bush which afforded us the opportunity to explore for days and weeks on end. We often searched for snakes (mostly red-belly black snakes) under pieces of iron or in the *leaf-litter* scattered around the bush. We didn't do anything with them except find them, disturb them a little and then runaway. It seemed like a dangerous thing to do which added to the enjoyment levels.

There also existed many irrigation dams, on many properties, which were *off-limits* to kids looking to swim in the hotter summer months. Although forbidden and could result in a substantial flogging for all concerned, those dams sure were refreshing and inviting when a *young one* needed to cool down. Who could want for more?

Chapter Twelve
The Chook House

'It's Always Funny Until Someone Gets Hurt'
(Quote: MUM)

One of the many games we played in the early days involved jumping off the "chook" shed roof landing in the surrounding long grass. Mum was always happiest when we were occupied doing our own things outside in the yard and not _under her feet_ inside. Afterall, she needed to concentrate on looking after the twins. Better still, when they slept, she could lie on her bed and read her _Mills & Boon_ romance novels: idyllic.

These *heady* afternoons of reading for Mum were only shattered when something serious happened to us whilst playing one of the many games we enjoyed.

I recall we climbed inside a *rusted-out* corrugated iron water tank lying next to the chook house, and rolled it up and down the driveway, which was brilliant. That is, until I stepped on the corroded edges and sliced my toes open, blood everywhere. We didn't wear shoes as we didn't own any (except ones for school). So, I raced inside and yelled out to Mum to let her know I'd cut my foot. She yelled back at me suggesting I should put a *band-aid* on it and get back outside to play. Good thinking.

When she wandered out of her bedroom and saw the pools of blood on the kitchen floor leading toward the bathroom door, she screamed and almost passed out. I was already back outside in the thick of the fun with my siblings. Thankfully, the cut wasn't as bad as the blood would have you think.

One of the funniest *chook house* memories occurred when Diane refused to jump off the roof, despite the protestations and urgings from Jude and me. We thought the rules of the game were simple: climb on the roof, count to three and jump but Diane had other ideas. She just refused. So ever the sympathetic siblings, Jude and I just pushed her off. *Outrageously funny* to us but obviously not so to Diane.

As we watched her crawl up the driveway on her elbows, like a commando on an ambush, we laughed even harder. She made it back to the house (about fifty metres) so we decided to call the game off as the ramifications could have been painful (for Jude and me). Luckily, Diane only sprained her ankle, and we were cleared of any *wrongdoing*. Disaster was thankfully averted yet again.

Some people just can't be told, I guess.

Chapter Thirteen
Little Kid Syndrome

'If You Want to Break It – Get an Axe'
(Quote: DAD)

've been told Dad bought me a tomahawk at the age of three as I was an industrious little fellow. I didn't talk but always managed to keep myself busy. This may have been an exasperated effort to stop me from climbing on the roof and sitting up there while Mum went into an emotional "melt-down" trying to entice me back down to *earth*. Or perhaps to try and stop me from running across the road to the neighbours with no clothes on or to even stop me from sitting in the huge *Mulberry Tree* which grew beside our house and laughing at Mum as she wished me down in one piece.

One of the fun things you can do with a small axe is cut your father's twenty metre power extension cord into thirty-centimetre lengths. Made sense to me but Dad was furious when he next needed to use the extension cord for one job or another. From memory though he didn't say much about that incident.

It was beginning to become clear to me that I had either inherited a previously dormant *Stupid Boy* gene or caught some form of disease that caused irresponsible and erratic behaviour. It clearly wasn't something demonstrated by my parents, siblings, or any other relatives across both sides of the family. It was obviously just *me*.

My favourite game with the tomahawk involved tying my eldest sister, Jude, to the clothesline and threatening to scalp her just like they did in the old *Cowboys and Indians* movies we had heard about when growing up. Again, just hours of fun and entertainment for everyone involved.

Anyway, it's also amazing how many trees you can cut down with a small axe, if you have patience. We used to roam around the bush and make *cubby houses* out of small trees; shrubs; dead branches and anything else we could find that afforded us some shelter, or a *hide-out* away from the prying eyes of our parents. We could then disappear from home for hours on end and have somewhere else to *hang out*. Surprisingly, Mum and Dad seemed to enjoy life considerably more in our absence: what an amazing thing to find out when you're only a kid. It did seem that this arrangement, however, suited every member of the family, except when things like bushfires emerged during the hotter summer months.

Not that our parents were overly concerned about the danger of fires, they were more concerned about who lit them. Well, it certainly wasn't us, or any of our friends from around the district, and certainly not by anyone from their families. The multitude of fires that regularly occurred must have been caused by visitors to the area or, maybe, lightning.

Medowie was, after all a small country town surrounded by thousands of acres of the Australian bush, and so fires were an inevitable part of growing up.

It was also no surprise to us that many of the adults in the area regularly started fires in a process they cleverly called *back-burning*. Getting rid of the grasses and scrub in the cooler months to reduce the severity of the inevitable fires in the summer months. So, it would be somewhat unfair to blame any (or all) of these fires on kids. Wouldn't it?

It must be said, too, that Dad was a *master* at *back-burning* operations to the point where we often sat at the tea table eating while grass fires raged around the acreage. This generally seemed to upset Mum much more than Dad, although he had to answer the knock at the door from the local *Volunteer Rural Fire Brigade* when they inevitably arrived.

Dad said in the end it was just easier to join up as a volunteer. That was, until they realised, he was a *borderline pyromaniac* who enjoyed lighting fires more than extinguishing them.

$\diamond$

Chapter Fourteen
Rusty the Wonder Dog

'In Life, True Friends Are Hard to Find'
(Quote: ME)

After the tomahawk episode, Mum and Dad decided to gift me a dog, all for myself, perhaps in the belief that this would distract me from my dangerous, emerging behaviours.

So, enter Rusty: my very own *mixed breed* cattle dog. I loved my dog. We played together and I fed him and spent so much time with him. I think my siblings were secretly jealous that I had my very own pet, and it was a dog, too, not just a pathetic ordinary pet.

Jude and Diane had a pet chicken called Softy but that was nothing like having your own dog: now that's a REAL pet. Whilst on the subject of Softy, it should be noted that the chook was often placed in a pram whilst my sisters walked it down to Muir's shop across the road, like a real baby (oh dear). When Softy got a bit too old to be a pet, Dad finally killed it.

Mum served it for dinner one night and it tasted just fine. Perfect roast chicken for all. Of course, we mentioned this to Jude and Diane during the meal amid much mirth and laughter. Jude's response "... Michael, you're such a pathological liar ..." and Diane chipped in "... yes Michael, shut up ..." They were still holding on to the line Mum and Dad peddled where "Softy the Chook" was taken by a fox, and to support this lie Dad replaced it with a rather "awkward looking substitute", which didn't really look anything like Softy, anyway.

To this day the girls won't believe we ate their pet for dinner. but we know the real 'truth'.

Best chicken dinner ever from my point of view.

Anyway, back to Rusty. He was perfect in every way, and as I wasn't old enough to start primary school yet, he did give me the distraction Mum and Dad craved for me in life. I've always imagined Rusty and me on holidays together, walking along the beach, frolicking in the surf, and calling into the Butchers shop on the way home. Or running through the bush chasing birds and lizards before returning home at the end of a long day for dinner. Idyllic days creating beautiful memories indeed.

About 12 months later Rusty ran away.

What a kick in the nuts for a little kid growing up in the Australian bush. It obviously created some hilarious moments and memories for my siblings who loved watching me "crash" back down to earth. I was becoming way too smug; happy and self-satisfied for their liking.

Anyway, back to my stupid ways after a small respite from reality.

Chapter Fifteen
Time to Get Back to Work

'The Harder You Work the Luckier You Get'
(Quote: DAD)

As we settled further into the gentle rhythm of home life, my siblings and I were finally all enrolled at Medowie Primary School and thus began the next stage of childhood. Mum knew it was time to get back to work as money was incredibly tight even though as a family our needs were limited. In fact, our fellow residents in Medowie were generally all beautiful people of *limited means* so we never felt different or like we were *missing out*.

Many of Mum and Dad's friends from Medowie were employed in, or around, the RAAF Base at Williamtown in various service roles. These included cooking, cleaning and service jobs in a variety of locations so it didn't take long for Mum to secure a position at the Airman's Mess or *Canteen* as it was known.

With employment came the need for a second car and the gruelling task of Mum getting a driver's licence - oh boy that must have been hard for her. Realistically, Mum was never *comfortable* driving, but given she had to return to work and Dad used the car for his work (despite many months of riding a bicycle to and from) it was inevitable. The fact too, that the kids now played weekend sport (not always in Medowie either) our family couldn't really have survived without two active drivers.

Suffice to say, I think it was a little easier to get a driver's licence back in the day. Mum was promoted immediately to the post of '... *the family's most reluctant, second most needed, sometimes and only if Dad was busy ...*' driver. She did fit the role perfectly I must say.

With the added responsibility of being the second driver came little or no extra time to get things done around the house, so Mum came to rely more and more on her children. I suspect this didn't quite work out as well for her as she may have expected. Anyway, we tried, but as they say in the classics '... *shit happens ....*'.

One of the huge advantages to us as kids, however, was that whenever Mum worked at the RAAF Base we could tag along and use some of the facilities. The swimming pool was one of the biggest drawcards for us in the summer. So too, the picture theatre, where movies were played on Friday, Saturday, and Sunday nights at a cost of five cents each. Low enough for our whole family to enjoy new movie releases on an occasional basis.

Another huge advantage with Mum's new work occurred during school holidays. We were lucky enough to be able to go to the RAAF Base and, as mentioned, swim or go to the pictures or just muck around in a different environment which was great.

One of the best things on offer though was to be allowed to travel on the "Tucker Van" which was driven around the Base by Val. She sold hot food, drinks, biscuits, pastries, and other such delights to the RAAF Personnel for morning tea or lunch.

Of course, it was mandatory that we tried the cream buns, or pies and sausage rolls, or even just a bag of chips. Best school holidays ever when you lucked out and travelled on the food truck. Mind you, it wasn't uncommon to struggle getting back into the school uniform after a couple of weeks of this enjoyment but, you know, someone had to do it.

Chapter Sixteen
Over-Active Imaginations

'Idle Hands Are the Devil's Work'
(Quote: UNKNOWN)

Kids can be an inventive bunch. We loved games like *home judo* where the bigger sibling got to throw the smaller siblings around in the name of sport. You could only play if you wore a dressing gown and left your brain in the kitchen before a matchup. Not sure who invented it but, given that I was *bigger and older* than Ray and

Muriel, I suspect I enjoyed the game far more than the other *willing* participants. In an attempt to woo others to play my "games", I would talk up the benefits and assure all participants that no one would get hurt. Ray's response was often short and to the point "... I just don't believe anything you tell me, Michael ..." and often Muriel's response would be more cautious but similar "... you're so funny Michael, even your lies make me laugh ..." We all played regardless and, occasionally, some of us would actually get hurt.

Circus acts always got a run and provided hours of endless entertainment fun and frivolity. Making your younger sister Muriel stand against a tree with arms outstretched whilst I threw a tomahawk or darts at her was heaps of fun for most of the participants. Climbing the water tower or the mulberry tree and not falling off was a bit like a high wire act. So was spitting on people from these dizzying heights as they walked below, although far less popular. Juggling involved the use of fruit (obviously) but this met with limited success. *Hide & Go Seek* was also a cracker. On my turn, I loudly counted to ten then, just sat down to watch TV. They eventually came out of hiding and realised I was just *taking the piss*. I thought it was hilarious, but not so my brother and sisters.

Playing billiards or snooker on a blanket on the kitchen table with apples and oranges for balls was also fun. Saucepans on chairs for pockets and a broomstick for a cue stick generally sufficed. Hours of family fun until our parent's realised the fruit was always bruised or rotten which brought a swift halt to that brilliant game.

Although I guess our greatest pleasure came from card games or board games. The five of us could ruthlessly play the one game of *Monopoly* for five days (before and after school) but each game always ended the same way: with Dad coming home from work, picking the board up and throwing it across the room. He hated the fact that we always argued, fought, and whinged. We all cheated too, but hey, that's what kids' games are for aren't they?

Squatter, Risk, The Game of Life, Scrabble, Yahtzee, were also games of choice. Drawing cartoon characters and playing word games out of a dictionary or thesaurus was also popular. Card games such as *Euchre, 500, Bridge, Cribbage* and *Oh Hell* provided enormous hours of fun for the whole family too, as well as the many guests and visitors who joined in when gracing our home with their presence.

In the end, Dad decided to purchase a *three-quarter* size Billiard Table which became a huge focus of our growing lives, from childhood and adolescence through to adulthood. It provided hours upon hours of fun for us all, including a steady stream of our friends, cousins, aunts, and uncles and many of Mum and Dads friends from around the district.

The billiard table was used on an almost daily basis during school holidays, Christmas, and Easter *breaks* by an array of people. The hours and hours of fun enjoyed were such that it is still one of the highlights of our lives when reflecting on family life and childhood.

Later in life, Mum and Dad decided to "down-size" and sell the family home and move to a smaller property about a kilometre away, but still in Medowie. As Dad didn't want to offend any of his children he disposed of the billiard table after cutting it into pieces with an axe. He just cut it up and threw it away. He then didn't have to decide who to give it to, or listen to any of us complain, because we *missed out* on being *gifted* the table. Strangely enough, none of us were really worried about it and he could have given it to any of his children without any fuss. Such was the mindset obviously permeating through the Stewart genes however, he decided that the destruction of the table was the *best option.*

Other favourite pastimes as we grew towards out teenage years involved meeting at the local telephone box located on the main road in front of our house and adjacent to Muir's shop. Perfect for just hanging out and making the odd prank phone call just for a laugh.

Our two favourites firstly involved ringing a *random number* and asking if Mr Wall was there? After the answer of '... *no* ...' we asked if Mrs Wall was there? Again '... *no* ...', so finally are there any Walls there? With obviously the answer being '... *no* ...'. Our witty reply? '... *Well, you'd better run out of the house before the roof falls down* ....'. Hilarious, I know. The second involved calling a *random Butchers Shop* and asking if they had pig's feet or trotters? Presumably the answer would be '... *yes* ...' as it was a Butcher's Shop after all. Our cutting response was always, '.... *Well, if you wear socks then no one will notice* ...' Sparkling wit and repartee all round we thought. Just a bit of fun really.

Chapter Seventeen
Punishment

'*You Always Seem to Cop It in The End*'
(Quote: ME)

Being a member of a large family of *limited means*, came with a range of responsibilities. You eat what you're served or go without, you do your chores before and after school, you're expected to become "self-sufficient" to a point, and you basically just "... do as you're told, and we'll all get along just fine ..." This is one area of life where I struggled: a lot.

When it was time for the kids to clean up after dinner, wash and dry the dishes and put everything away, I often developed stomach cramps and needed to go to the toilet - quickly. This worked for a time but eventually the others would stop and wait for me to come out of the 'loo. They didn't want me to miss out on the fun. I needed some new strategies.

In fairness, we were all active kids with wonderful imaginations, so we sort of didn't like rules much at all. We strangely detested punishment even more. Over the years, a pattern or theme was developed by Mum when it came to finding the "guilty one". This became far too predictable after a while and therefore suited us perfectly (almost all of us, anyway).

Mum would shout at us, threaten us with violence by Dad when he got home from work, take out her weapon of choice (usually a wooden spoon or spatula), line us up in order of age and then start by whacking Jude, then Diane, then me, then Ray, then Muriel, then return to the top of the line. She would ask again "... who did it; who broke it; who stole it; etc etc ..." and without fail, Diane would say it was her before Mum started the second round of punishment.

The funny part was, Diane was never guilty she just hated being whacked.

To add some spice to this charade I often found Mum's *weapons of choice* and buried them somewhere randomly in the yard, which obviously made the punishment routine even funnier. Such was the tenacity of our mother however, she always managed to find a 'new' weapon to whack us with and so the process of burying continued for many years.

It should be noted that, although Mum threatened severe punishment and violence against her children, she never really followed through in anyway. Ok, the occasional whack with some handy kitchen utensils but nothing serious. If those threats didn't work, there was always the "... wait till your father gets home from work ..." comment.

Mum's last resort. Except, funnily enough, Dad never whacked us anyway. That wasn't his style at all really.

He would maybe get the belt which was hanging behind the bedroom door as a threat, stand over you and say "... ok, this is going to hurt me more than it's going to hurt you ..." to which I would often mumble "... I find that hard to believe ..." This was always very scary, but I can't recall too much damage being inflicted by Dad and his belt. He would often use humour to calm everyone down or show some "overwhelming" disappointment so we would feel bad. Mostly, though, he was more likely to just call us *bloody idiots* or, (in my case), *Stupid Boy*.

Another great idea I brought to reality, only once though, happened when I lost a tooth. We knew that as our "baby teeth" fell out you could leave them in a glass of water in the kitchen overnight and in the morning the *Tooth Fairy* had taken the tooth and replaced it with a five-cent coin.

There had to be an angle here to make some money, so one night whilst waiting for the *Tooth Fairy*, I wandered out into the kitchen and noticed "she" had already been (we were always told the *Tooth Fairy* was female). So, I picked up the five-cent coin, put it in Mum's purse and took out a ten-cent coin, and then placed that on the kitchen bench next to the glass of water. In the morning, I was ecstatic, my siblings jealous, and Mum and Dad were very confused, probably because they knew the *Tooth Fairy* always only ever left five cents. They looked at me but said nothing. Profitable night all round I thought.

Anyway, I'd like to think we were *normal* kids who pushed a few boundaries. Maybe, deep down, I knew we were far worse than that at times: little *shits* may be a more apt description.

Thankfully Mum and Dad loved us, and they both had a (very) high tolerance level.

The Big Linen Cupboard

'No One Likes a Smart Arse, Michael'
(Quote: MUM & DAD)

Despite there being many house extensions undertaken by Dad over the years, one of the BIG ONES involved a new laundry and toilet. Much needed for such a large family I must say.

Our toilet was originally a *pan-style* in the *dunny* situated in the back yard about fifty metres from the house. Common in Australia up to the 1960s and 1970s, this type of toilet involved a visit by a *waste collector* weekly who emptied the pan into a *waste truck* and replaced the used pan with a *sterilised* one, which was then placed back in the outdoor *dunny*.

Dad decided an improvement was required. He dug a trench through the road with a shovel and mattock (about 200 metres) and connected our house to the reticulated water supply. He then constructed an extension outside the back door of the house which included a toilet, large laundry and big 'floor to ceiling' linen storage cupboard (state-of-the-art for the 1970s I'm sure). Mum was thrilled, and this proved to be a brilliant precursor to the removal of the rooftop water tank in favour of a new connection to the reticulated water supply in Medowie.

I remember having a bit of an argument with Mum about some major issue and she politely suggested I go out and play and don't come back till teatime. I thought this was a shit idea, so I thought I'd go and hide in the new linen cupboard. The horizontal shelves were far enough apart for me to lie down and pass the time reflecting on my life (or something equally important I have no doubt).

After about four hours I jumped out and went to toilet. I know, that's a long time to lie in a cupboard doing nothing believe me. After another couple of hours, I heard some movement in the laundry and the washing machine startup, so I imagined my chance was drawing ever closer. Then everything went quiet again -patience my son -patience.

Half an hour later I heard some more noise and (what sounded like) clothes being taken out of the machine so Mum would have been hanging the washing out. The sliding door started to OPEN. It was Mum about to put some towels in the cupboard right near my head. I screamed out *BOO* and laughed and laughed. Mum almost had a heart attack and was VERY UNIMPRESSED, furious might be a better description, but I just thought that was *'piss funny'* and genius.

Like a crocodile waiting in disguise for its prey -I attacked seven hours after setting up in my camouflaged position in the cupboard. *Stupid Boy* strikes again.

✧

Chapter Nineteen
Religion / Sunday School

'Don't Forget, It's Not Always About You, Michael'
(Quote: MUM & DAD)

ike most families in the 1960s and 1970s, religion played a role in the growth and development of the "core" family unit. As kids we were expected to attend Church on Sunday mornings (Anglican was our religion of choice I believe). Strangely the five kids always managed the twenty-minute walk on our own as our parents were generally a *bit busy*. Funny thing that.

Anyway, we dressed appropriately and tucked a five-cent coin into our pockets and walked to the Anglican Church for the morning service. This was closely followed by a second session called "Sunday School". This session was reserved for kids and was hosted by our school principal's daughter, Miss Earp. We listened to plenty of stories about Jesus and his crew, coloured in pamphlets and generally gave Mum and Dad a few hours peace back at home.

I worked out the real action in Church was during the first session. It included the "more important" stories and songs (called hymns) and we sat and listened as the Father worked through them all until the end of the program, about an hour into the session. This is where the five-cent coin comes into play.

A large plate was handed around with the expectation that the assembled *parishioners* would leave *donations* to the Church in the plate, and therefore, by implication, to God. Made sense, I guess. The Father had, after all, spent hours relating tales to us from the Bible and convincing us to stay on the "straight and narrow" lest eternal damnation would befall us all, so you would assume he needed to be paid for his services.

So, I figured if I rattled my five-cent coin on the plate and was quick enough, I could take a coin OFF the plate without anyone noticing. Genius (morally corrupt but genius for a kid). I could then spend the spoils at the shop on the way home and everyone would be "none-the-wiser". So good was my plan, in fact, I couldn't see anything possibly going wrong, and it didn't. Not sure what I spent the five cents on but I'm sure it was delicious.

My brother and sisters were having none of this no matter how genius they thought it. Mum and Dad were told, and I copped an absolute flogging for this one. I never did it again.

A stupid idea for a *Stupid Boy* which, really, just amounted to "theft", I've been led to believe.

Chapter Twenty
Broken Lounge

'Michael, You're A Bloody Idiot'
(Quote: DAD)

As you know, money was tight back in the day and our parents saved incredibly hard anytime something had to be purchased for the home. Items such as furniture or white goods were very expensive, and months and months of saving was required (and therefore going without something else) to make a new purchase possible.

We remember the prized, brown, *faux-leather* lounge Mum and Dad saved "so hard for" to purchase in the 1970s. A real showpiece that was displayed front and centre in the lounge room opposite the television.

This was inevitably our parents' favourite location to relax whilst the kids sat on the floor. Typical 1970s household I'd say.

Only months after purchase we were skylarking outside (most likely at Raymond's insistence) and some bright spark decided it was time to run inside and watch some TV.

Being the bully I was, I pushed the others out of the way and ran in and jumped on the prized lounge suite to get the best viewing spot. The timber back leg of the lounge snapped off and we all wound up on the floor. What an absolute disaster.

Thinking on my feet, I rushed outside, grabbed two bricks, and slid them under the back corner of the lounge. Repositioned it perfectly and threw the broken timber leg away. No disaster at all really, just a bad situation made better by some clever quick thinking. Or so I thought.

Two weeks later Mum was vacuuming the floor and moved the lounge to get behind it. She screamed at the top of her lungs as the corner of the lounge fell on to her foot and nearly broke it. Even Diane wouldn't own up to this one. In fact, even though I could normally "garner" some support from at least a couple of my siblings, this time, I was *toast*.

Thankfully Diane offered a little support when she suggested "... Michael, maybe you should have thought a bit harder before running in and smashing yourself onto the lounge ..."

Stupid Boy copped another "well-deserved" flogging and felt the full wrath of both parents this time around. To make matters worse, Mum lectured me "... Michael, why do you do these things? No one else makes the mistakes you make, and they certainly think before they do something stupid, but not you. Why, oh why, can't you just be like the other kids? ..." You could genuinely see her heart breaking as the words escaped her lips.

It took a while for us to all move on after this little episode.

Chapter Twenty-One
My 10ᵗʰ Birthday

**'I'm Not Stupid –
It's Just the Way They Dress Me'**

(Quote: MUM)

This was shaping as the event of the year in Medowie: my 10th birthday which included a REAL PARTY for the first time in my life. The anticipation was electric.

I assumed I had friends at school (despite the total enrolment of students at Medowie Primary being sixty-one from kindergarten through to sixth class) so my parents had a chance to invite quite a few kids to enjoy our little soirée. Mum and Dad arranged some invitations early because my birthday is in January which was during the Christmas School holidays.

We made some streamers out of crepe paper with scissors and glue and decided to hang them in the carport: the scene of the party. We moved the table out there as well and spent a bit of time setting up the venue to make it look spectacular. I was VERY excited.

We thought a start around two o'clock made sense. The kids could *pig out* all afternoon on some goodies, and play a few games, before heading home around 4:30 p.m. in time for dinner. Mum asked me to have a bath and tidy up at twelve o'clock: it was like living in a dream.

I washed my bits and combed a heap of *Brylcreem* through my hair (*product* or *gel* for the *young ones*) and dressed in shorts, T-shirt, thongs and my favourite yellow cardigan with brown buttons and *cable-stitch* to the left-hand and right-hand sides down the front. Looking *real smooth* if I must say so myself.

I sat and waited with a little cardboard party hat on my head and surveyed the spoils across the table. We had the odd streamer and balloon around the carport to enhance the amazing party atmosphere.

I sat and waited a bit more: happy in the knowledge that most kids had to walk to get to our place as there was no public transport in Medowie back in those days, so no rush. I sat and waited a lot longer. It was only three o'clock and the type of food we had scattered around the table wasn't likely to spoil. I thought about starting a game in anticipation of some kids arriving but, as they say, '… *it pays to be patient* …'. That's easy to say but geez it's hard when you're just a ten-year-old kid.

Mum came out to see me around four o'clock and said "... *Michael, maybe you should go and get changed - I don't think anyone's coming ...*". I was obviously gutted but didn't say anything. I got up, took off my little party hat, my yellow cardigan with the brown buttons and walked inside to get changed.

I thought that maybe, just maybe, there'd been a mishap with the invitations. Sadly, though, I knew the reality was such that I'd had a birthday party, and no one turned up (not even my brother and sisters) but I guess they were very busy that day.

At least we had dinner sorted.

✧

Chapter Twenty-Two
Bushmasters Craft Lessons

'Keeping Young Boys Busy
Whilst Learning New Skills'

(Quote: ME)

S hortly after the debacle of my 10th birthday *no show*, Dad thought I'd enjoy a new distraction by joining the local *Bushmasters Craft Group* which had recently commenced in the area. Back in the day, this group held weekly meetings at the Williamtown Local Hall near the RAAF Base about 10 kilometres from home. I thought it was worth a try. I mean '... *what could possibly go wrong ...*'?

I was very keen to get to *Bushmasters* to see if I could pick up a few extra skills. I was already proficient in the use of the tomahawk Dad gave me when I was three years old. I was also keen, loved getting lost in the bush and knew how to light fires: valuable skills indeed.

Apparently, the group offered badges to the kids to recognise their achievements along similar lines to other groups operating across Australia at the time. These included a variety of options across a *set program*. Kids could pick and choose along the way (based on their interests) to ultimately find new ways to express themselves as they navigated through life.

Mum and Dad seemed happy to see me doing something *constructive* away from home given my history of being a *very very difficult child* at home. In short, the distraction for me may have also improved the lives of those in my family.

Anyway, I decided to *play to my strengths* and go a bit *left field*. Rather than learning some trivial skills like *Building a Safe Campfire* or *Using a Compass in the Bush*, I looked to improve my skill set with something a more stimulating and "extreme".

No one at home really asked me how things were going after each meeting which was fine - I merely concentrated on learning something new for the sake of learning something new, and hoped in the end they would all be surprised at my increased knowledge and skills.

After (what seemed) just a short six weeks I was awarded my first ever *Arm Badge*. You could imagine the surprise on the faces of everyone when they realised it was the first ever for any kid in the *Bushmasters Craft Group* too, which is high praise indeed. I had attained a high level of proficiency in the rare skill of *'Hide the Sausage'*. My *Skill Leader* was so proud. Mum and Dad somewhat less (I later found out). That must be why I can't recall returning to learn additional skills with the group and wasn't given the chance to attempt the next level in that extremely challenging *Arm Badge Series*.

Anyway, I reluctantly moved on to try my hand at some other childhood pursuits.

Chapter Twenty-Three
The Freedom of The Open Road

'It Only Hurts When You Land'

(Quote: ME)

Dad was a *Junior Road Cycling Champion* when he was growing up in Far North Queensland. Not that he spoke about this achievement much, but he did know heaps about riding and repairing bicycles. A skill he put to good use as we were growing up in Medowie.

By the age of about nine, maybe ten, we were privileged to be given a bike. These were usually *hand me downs* from cousins or friends of the family and that was when Dad would go to work. He repaired the 'new' bike, checked tyres and inner tubes, oiled and / or repaired the chain, made sure we had a bike pump and often painted them to give them a little *personal touch*. Not sure we appreciated this as much then as now, but the bike did, at least, provide us with more freedom after school and on the weekends.

Once we mastered the skill of riding, we were also allowed to ride to school. Most of our friends were also allowed to ride so the trips to and from school often became more fun than the actual school day. Medowie enjoyed huge areas of bushland and therefore plenty of scope for bike riders to find trails to get away from the roads and the *prying eyes* of parents. So much fun, so little time.

On one of my usual bike rides to school I caught up with a few of my *mates* who had to ride past our home to get to school. Uneventful as the ride was, I suggested we catch up for the ride home too. Safety in numbers so to speak and hopefully a bit more fun than riding on your own. Anyway, three o'clock rolled around and we jumped on our *pushies* to pedal the few kilometres home from school.

The group I rode with were generally considered the "cool kids" of the school, in sixth class and the oldest at the school. I thought I was probably making a move to the "cooler side of life" by joining in for the ride home. There was only about five of us as we made our way up the small hill toward the *Medowie Hall* before turning to the right onto the "main road" (not really a busy road but it was called "Main Road" none-the-less).

As we rounded the corner someone yelled out "…. let's race down the hill …." which seemed like a challenge too good to resist. We rode as a bunch and after about 400 metres there was little between us – *neck and neck* would be an apt description. David looked to his left and I was almost level with him as we hit the bottom of the hill and crossed the *culvert* over the creek. David, the "self-confessed" leader of the group, hated getting beat so he lashed out with his left leg and pushed me off the roadway, off my bike and into the bush next to the creek. He slowed briefly and then absolutely *pissed himself* laughing, rode off and caught up with Kevin, one of the other "cool ones", to relay his hilarious story about kicking me into the bush.

I hit the ground hard as I left the road and rolled down the two metre drop to the creek. My bike flew up in the air after smashing into the rocks next to the creek and I finally came to a stop about five metres away from both my bike and the edge of the embankment next to the roadway. As I stood up, I noticed I had blood pouring out me everywhere and felt like my head was about to explode. My bike was also the worse for wear, with a severely bent front wheel, loose handlebars, and a flat rear tyre. I managed to drag myself up to the road with my bike on my shoulder and slowly started to walk the remaining kilometre home.

So much for a fun ride home from school.

It was about then that I stopped wondering why no one showed up at my 10th Birthday Party. Obviously not quite as popular a kid as I'd always hoped I'd be, and certainly hadn't made any inroads towards being one of the "cooler kids at school".

You can't have everything you want in life, I guess.

$\Diamond$

Chapter Twenty-Four
Christmas in Medowie

'It's Always Better to Give Than Receive (Apparently)'
(Quote: UNKNOWN)

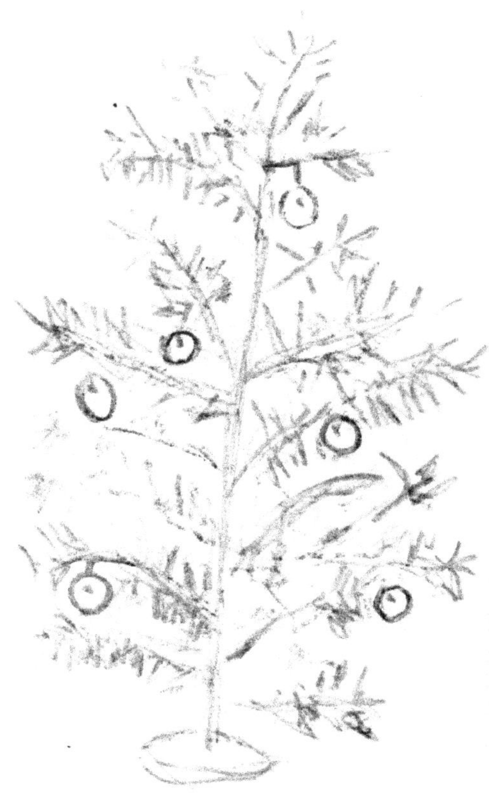

Truly one of the most wonderful times of year for everyone. School *break* was generally six weeks of summer bliss. Playing cricket; watching cricket, staying up a bit late and watching television, catching up with the other kids around town and generally just having some fun.

Mum and Dad were more relaxed too. Friends would often drop in and basic (but thoughtful) gifts exchanged which added that "feel good" element to the season. There was also a constant stream of grandparents, aunts; uncles and cousins coming and going which made it very busy and from time-to-time we'd be "on the road" visiting all of them too.

I think this helped Mum (in particular) cope better with the burden of raising so many kids, working, also managing, a household. Christmas was like a bit of *time-out* for everyone.

Our Christmas Tree was sourced from the bush up the back, cut down and dragged home, before standing it up in a twenty litre can with some gravel and water. The tree was then decorated by us, and the lounge room could be dedicated as *Christmas Central* for a month or so. Nothing fancy mind you, just a few pieces of tinsel, balloons, crepe paper streamers, and some handmade decorations, which varied from year-to-year.

The one thing every "bush" kid can remember about a Christmas like this is the *smell* of the tree. Commonly a eucalyptus or casuarina straight out of the bush which, if lucky, would last a couple of weeks before it dried out completely. It was wonderful.

Mum and Dad would put aside a few dollars for presents throughout the year, and if Mum found anything *on sale* (cheap) when shopping she would put that to one side and keep it to give as a gift to someone at Christmas. In a household of limited means, Christmas gifts were still a big deal, so what may have been lacking in cost was more than compensated for in quantity. We spent weeks, even months, wrapping, writing on name tags and adding to the pile of presents under the tree to the point there was limited room to sit and watch television.

Christmas Day dawned warm and still, with the temperature in the mid-thirty degrees, but the pace inside the house was frenetic. Not supposed to be out of bed before six o'clock in the morning, but we knew that rule was relaxed a little given our levels of excitement. Opening presents was the priority but we usually flicked on some "Christmas Carols" and grabbed some chocolate before the organised chaos began.

We opened 1 gift at a time, just like death by a thousand cuts. Muriel selected first and gave that to the designated owner, then after they opened the gift, they picked the next one for someone else and so on. Weird I know, but everyone got to see who received what, and from whom, even though it could take up to four hours. This was a brilliant way to spend Christmas morning together as one family but did take plenty of patience.

Ever the generous, giving one, I collected every scrap of the wrapping paper, cardboard, gift tags and any other rubbish lying around and took it all outside to help clean the lounge room. That's the sort of helpful child I was. The incinerator was setup behind the garage, near the side fence, so I whacked a fair bit of rubbish in and lit it up (with just a hint of petrol to ensure it kicked off). The outside temperature was hovering around thirty-five degrees, and there was a strong breeze, but I kept piling on the cardboard and paper and made a massive fire. This was how I liked my fires: big and "out-of-control".

In a flash, the grass along the fence line caught on fire then the back of the weatherboard shed. I was sweating big time as I tried to control this inferno. Should I run inside and get help or battle on to save any embarrassment? An hour later I had it all under control with a garden hose, washed my hands, ignored the scorched grass and blackened rear wall of the shed and casually walked back inside for some breakfast. No one even noticed I'd been gone (which was not uncommon I must say).

Lucky doesn't begin to describe the outcome of this potential disaster I'd created.

Stupid Boy the pyromaniac had struck again.

Chapter Twenty-Five
Happy New Year

'The Painful Side of Gluttony'

(Quote: ME)

uckily for me, I struggled to get into (too much) trouble at this time of the year - I just stayed away from home from breakfast till almost dark. Whether playing next door with the Galloways or playing cricket and hanging out across the road with the Muirs', life was truly idyllic with little or no responsibility.

I did still manage to break things, but it seemed less of a *hassle* and a bit more relaxed around home at this time of the year. I hated visiting cousins, aunts and uncles but genuinely looked forward to catching up with Nan and Pop at Stockton. Nan and I were happiest fishing down near the ferry wharf. Pop just loved giving you cash to buy things from Lewis's shop, and I was allowed to go to the pictures (movies) on my own. As I got older, I was trusted to run to the TAB to put bets on the horses for them both. Just loving life really.

Fishing on the *Ferry Wharf* at Stockton was such a relaxing pastime for Nan and me. I recall borrowing one of Dad's fishing rods to take to Nan's to enhance the fishing experience one Christmas, with Dad's blessing. As the ferry streamed in toward the wharf, I tripped and kicked the rod over the side into the water, never to be seen again. Sadly, when I got home and told Dad, he looked at me for a minute or two, and then said "... you're a bloody idiot Michael. How can you lose a fishing rod on the wharf ...?" Welcome to my world.

Generally, though, at this time of the year, Jude and Diane would stay at an aunt and uncles house for a week, and Raymond and Muriel would stay at another relatives' place, so it was a win all round for the entire family. Fortunately, one year though, both Raymond and I visited Nan and Pop together, and we had an eventful five days enjoying the best Stockton had to offer.

Pop was a funny old bloke. He loved his geese (which were pests who attacked everyone and anyone) and he loved Crossword Puzzles. Didn't mind the odd beer or two (usually no more though) and did he love his food. In fact, he was a *gastronomic pig*. We could watch him eat for hours and always got a laugh out of his antics. His major problem however was that he was such a pig he rarely, if ever, chewed his food.

On one of the nights during our stay, Nan served him his favourite dish, fresh grilled fish (caught that day by us I must say). Pop in his usual fashion *wolfed* it down, had dessert, and went to bed early, as he often did. Early the next morning all hell seemed to have broken loose in the house.

There were screams, much shouting and plenty of running around as Nan and Pop rushed into the bathroom and slammed the door. Ray and I stood and watched, unsure whether to stay or go outside, or just wait it out and watch television. The screams grew louder, there was plenty of swearing, then silence from the bathroom. About five minutes later this cycle started again, and the *show* continued along these lines for another thirty minutes or so. We were mesmerised, frozen to the floor outside of the bathroom door, where we just waited and wondered.

After another few minutes, the door slowly opened, Pop walked out with tears streaming down his face, head hanging slightly to the side and then looked up and said to us both, "... *if you ever get a fish bone caught in your arse boys, never get it outwith tweezers ...*". He walked off and went back to bed and we didn't see him until the next day. We laughed until the tears streamed down our cheeks and told Nan she deserved a medal. Her actions went way beyond what would normally be expected in any marriage.

As an aside I always remember Nan as a down-to-earth woman who enjoyed a smoke and some brandy to pass the time of day. She enjoyed a wicked sense of humour and loved her grandkids to bits. Unfortunately, though, as she aged her eyesight failed her, to the point she was legally blind by the time I was about nine or ten years old.

Fiercely independent, she refused to move out of her home where she had happily lived for many years. It was always scary watching her make a cup of tea or cook meals in the kitchen. She had a gas stove and would light one of the cookers on the top to boil the kettle. Not knowing which of the burners she had lit, though, meant that she had to run her hand over the top of the stove until she found the one that was hot.

What a beautiful woman was Nan.

Chapter Twenty-Six

Family Holidays

**‘Even Stupid Boy Deserves a Break,
Doesn't He?’**

(Quote: ME)

We were lucky enough to enjoy a week away on holidays as a family once a year. Dad usually booked some modest accommodation in a small town on the east coast, somewhere north of Newcastle, in the Spring or Summer months. We could then pass the time swimming at the beach or doing a little bit of fishing, exploring or making mischief.

Towns like Yamba, South West Rocks, North Haven, Laurieton, Forster, Soldiers Point or even Taylors Beach spring to mind and each

80

was equally as enjoyable. We could just run around all day, have fun, and eat lunch and dinner from any of the local shops so the atmosphere was always idyllic.

Sometimes Mum would work and drive to our destination later, on her own, or we would all travel together in the station wagon playing games like *Eye-Spy, I Hate Your Guts* or even *See How Long You Can Shut-Up*. An entertaining six hours in the car for all.

On some occasions our aunties, uncles and cousins would join us for a few days, or the whole week, which was great: the more the merrier we found. They not only provided a distraction for us kids, but gave Mum and Dad some adult company, time to play cards at night, and enjoy a few alcoholic beverages without the kids getting under their feet for the entire week.

Dad, in particular, loved the week off work as it gave him a chance to go fishing (with an uncle or two on some occasions which made it even better), relax with the kids and spend a bit of time at the beach. Mum, too, was able to kick back and relax because she didn't have to worry about the *never-ending* stream of housework that needed to be sorted back at home.

On one holiday, when I was about eight years old, I was proudly showing off my new wristwatch, which was given to me by Santa a month or so earlier. Leather band, silver surrounds and a polished glass face, it was top of the range for a young kid. I thought I was *fashion personified* on that holiday: chic and desperate for attention.

My siblings and I wandered down to the beach for a few hours on the second day of the holidays, hoping to soak up some sun, build a few sandcastles and generally relax in the waves. No hassles about cleaning our room, feeding the chooks, or doing the expected home chores: just peace and tranquillity. Bliss.

Ever the diligent one, I decided to secretly bury my watch in the sand so no one could steal my new jewellery accessory. Pretty smart thinking for an eight-year-old. So I could easily find it after my relaxing swim, I stuck a large stick in the sand to highlight the *magic* spot for the hidden treasure. In this way, I was assured of finding the watch later that morning.

Do you know how many sticks there are sticking up out of the sand on a beach?

I looked for that watch for hours but sadly couldn't find that special spot that seemed so identifiable before I ran to the water. My new possession was cruelly ripped from me through my own lack of common sense. *Stupid Boy* strikes yet again.

Mum and Dad were gutted (because they knew who Santa was and how much Santa had paid for that watch), but thankfully could see the logic in my thinking. So, whilst I wasn't flogged for this indiscretion, the pain of my stupidity lingered long. Sadly, I never received a watch for my birthday or Christmas ever again: funny thing that.

Chapter Twenty-Seven

School Christmas Play & Presentation

'Talent Always Seems to Shine Through'

(Quote: ME)

The entire last term of school each year was spent learning lines, preparing props, setting background scenes, and learning lines for the *Christmas Play*: heady stuff indeed. This was presented at night with parents, families, and friends in attendance, followed by the *Annual Presentation of Academic Awards*.

Our play in Year Six was titled *The Day They Landed* and to be honest it was a hoot. I was hoping to star in the show, but I didn't get a part. Mr Latimore wanted me to be the director (obviously setting a trap so I'd stuff up). I wasn't happy but had to work through it until the big night. We practiced a lot, and kids learnt their lines and we had a heap of fun getting ready for the big night. We hoped it would be worth the effort in the end.

The big night arrived and one of the *actors* (Jeffrey) didn't turn up: what to do? I had to step into the breach because I knew all the lines AND there was no one else. I played the part of *Sniffy* and only had to say '*... you little beauty ...*' towards the end of the play. What could possibly go wrong?

As it turned out, NOTHING.

The play was a hit, my line got a laugh, and everyone felt really great about themselves. I felt like I'd arrived without completely stuffing up.

A quick change and straight into speeches. First up, the Year Six kids had to try their hand at *Public Speaking* (we had prepared a little speech the week before) and so, full of confidence in front a huge crowd (for Medowie Primary School) I stepped on stage. Again, I *brained* it. My speech was well delivered and well received, so I was feeling very *chuffed* by this stage.

Down to the final two to see who would win first prize in the *Public Speaking* competition. It was just Valerie and me. Well, I'm *shitting bricks* at this stage, and I guess Valerie probably was as well. The final round included *Impromptu Speaking*. What did that mean?

Mr Earp (Headmaster) handed us both a card with some words on it and gave us one minute to work out what to say: the tension was mounting and the atmosphere palpable.

"Michael Stewart first", I heard Mr Earp say, as those words rang loudly in my ears. My topic: **'*The Australian Defence Force*'**.

Well, with an RAAF Base located 10 minutes down the road, and many of Medowie's residents being Defence Personnel, you'd think I'd "lucked out". Remember too that many other residents of Medowie worked in the Defence Support Services (like Mum and Dad) so this topic should have been *right up my alley*.

I walked up to the microphone, looked around, mentioned the name of my topic to the assembled crowd and looked around some more. I do recall mentioning Canberra, Federal Government and Army before I froze entirely. I looked up again, down to the ground and then up again. I then *peed my pants*. There was nothing left to do but look at the ground and just walk off the stage.

I don't remember hearing Valerie's speech, but she did a good job I was told. She did congratulate me, and so I tried to be magnanimous in defeat, however I needed to hurry off and get changed into some dry clothes.

Maybe I was finally being repaid for laughing so hard at Gai in Kindergarten who *peed* on the floor while drawing on the chalk board on the back wall.

Anyway, Valerie won the *Public Speaking Award*, and I received a *Participation Certificate*. I could always hang that next to the one they gave me at the *Annual Pet Show* with Freda the Friesian Cow back in third class.

Chapter Twenty-Eight
The End of Primary School

'All Good Things Must Come to an End'
(Quote: UNKNOWN)

So, the end of the year was fast approaching. The School Presentation was finished, School Reports had been handed to parents and the last week or so of the classroom was very relaxing for all involved. It dawned on the class that we were destined for High School in a few short months. Mr Earp spoke to us about what to expect and explained how we should look at our journey as an important part of growing and learning.

He told us how we were currently BIG frogs in a little pond, (the entire school had 61 enrolments) and next year we would become LITTLE frogs in an enormous pond (Raymond Terrace High School had over 1,100 enrolments). This meant that school life would be very different, and we would need to (basically) adapt to survive. Scary stuff indeed.

We were used to having the same teacher for at least two years in Primary School but would soon have a variety of teachers EACH DAY once in High School. Our lessons would be so different because each class had different teachers and, in some cases, different students so there was so much to learn, and it seemed very daunting.

We wandered out for lunch in a bit of a *daze* and played a few games. I hurried down to the *long jump* pit because I noticed Christine (who had been in my class since kindergarten), standing down around there. I was a bit keen on Christine and thought a bit of a chat might be in order. She watched me walk down and started to tell me how High School was going to be so different next year. She was excited and couldn't wait to meet some older "girls and guys" and just find some new friends, which I guess was a good attitude to have heading into this new and unknown environment called High School.

I thought we were sort of *boyfriend* and *girlfriend* in an 11year-old's way, and so I stood very close to her and tried to land a kiss on her cheek. She just laughed at me and then punched me in the face. Tears started to well in my eyes as she walked away, the thoughts and ideas in my head no longer fixated on a relationship. I realised I needed to ensure that I kept my distance into the future, because that punch bloody hurt: both my feelings and my face.

Stupid Boy had to finally move on into the big scary world of High School.

Chapter Twenty-Nine
Love Struck

'Wasting My Time Punching Above My Weight'
(Quote: UNKNOWN)

Wow - doesn't it hurt when you watch a goddess move into your family circle and the best you've got is no talent; you're devoid of personality; you have pimples; the *dress sense* of Sir Les Paterson and siblings who probably wished you were dead.

The sport of softball took off in our region and many of the families in Medowie (Boyds, Slobodniuks, Coxs, Stewarts, Muirs, etc) and the inevitable interest from families in Raymond Terrace (Studderts, Cotters, Peppers, etc) meant that almost every girl from ten to eighteen years old played weekly. This gave the young clowns like me a chance to get involved: well, just watch, really.

There was one amazing little cutie from the Studdert family who not only had talent but could have been painted by every Renaissance artist from the Middle Ages. I was VERY impressed with young Margaret, I must admit.

I had some issues however, apart from having one leg shorter than the other, nothing of size in my underpants, an unfortunate odour, no friends, and my age meant I was scorned and spat on by any girl older than me, I was still confident of connecting with Margaret. Yep, I wasn't the sharpest tool in the shed. It didn't help that most of the softball players were friends of my sisters, which relegated me immediately to *dirt-bag* status, at best, and realistically invisible, but I did dare to dream. What a *Stupid Boy*.

I watched every game of softball and genuinely hoped to be noticed by Margaret, but I think I was kidding myself, UNTIL one day I stood out in the crowd and no one could miss me. I accidentally shit my pants (sad but true). I wasn't hoping Margaret would notice me for anything other than my sparkling repartee, wit, keen sense of humour and an eye for softball, but instead I filled my dungarees with a brown mass of excrement: what a loser.

Suffice it to say she moved on quickly, although I had made an indelible impression. I'd hate to imply there was any interest from her but gee whiz, an eleven-year-old kid who can't control his bowels would have surely been a catch for any young girl making her way in life.

We did, however, cross paths a few years later with a mixed (perhaps more positive) outcome. Margaret was a year ahead of me at school so when I moved on to High School (Year Seven these days) she was in Year Eight, so I still thought I'd have a *crack*.

Around the latter part of my first year in High School, I summoned up a bit of courage and met Margaret outside Lab Five in the Science Block. The problem was I couldn't look at her because I was too shy. Instead, I spoke to her reflection in the window, and asked if she might like to catch up some time? Lame I know, but she did think about it: as she wandered off laughing quietly to herself without answering.

Stupid Boy never failed to make an impression.

Epilogue

'A Snapshot of Stupidity'

(ME)

That about sums up the first twelve years of my life. Masquerading as an intelligent human being all the while disguising my obvious lack of common sense and cherishing my stage name *Stupid Boy*. There were other disasters, events, triumphs, and stories but I've always felt a bit of an affinity with the ones I've included here.

You may wonder why my parents didn't just give me the name of *Stupid Boy* at birth instead of Michael? Well, my brother and sisters did ask Mum and Dad this question, on many occasions, and they always answered the same way: that name had already been used by Monte and Elsie from Williamtown for one of their sons. I've met that *Stupid Boy* many times and there is no doubt they nailed him: by name and by nature.

In fact, that *Stupid Boy* actually worked with my dad, Marshall, for almost thirty years. Let's call him Robert to avoid any confusion. So, in a way, Dad must have felt like he was surrounded by imbeciles (well a few imbeciles anyway) for most of his life.

It would be fair to say that Dad received little respite when he came home after a long hard day at work, given he had to (usually) sort out some problem I'd created in his absence. He had a big heart did Marshall.

Anyway, it would be great to be able to say that, as I aged, there were no other stories of incidents and accidents resulting from my *Stupid Boy* behaviour, but that would be wrong. To even be able to say that I improved somewhat and made fewer dumb decisions would be a positive, but that, too, would be a lie.

My life generally continued along a similar pattern for many more years. Most of my behaviour from the ensuing years, sadly, still follows the common theme displayed in the stories detailed above. So, as I grew older, I slowly came to the realisation that I could no longer be considered a *Stupid Boy*. I had graduated to the next major *milestone* in the whirlpool of life: I became a *Stupid Teenager*.

Oh, and it is probably only fair to you, the reader, to reveal which of the tales detailed in the chapters above are true; partly true, or outright lies. Afterall, I did indicate at the beginning that ".... *some of these stories may actually be true* ..." So, in a *blow-by-blow* expose, I'm happy to advise as follows:-

Chapter One - A Growing Family on the Move. True but with a little
bit of hyperbole thrown in to make it sound more exciting, but
true all the same;

Chapter Two – Medowie the Amazing 'Melting Pot'. True although I didn't get *"...kicked up the arse ..."* by many people to be honest, although I have been told I probably should have been;

Chapter Three – Back to My Real Birth. Completely True. Mum and Dad were definitely advised that I wouldn't make it through the birth but, in the end, happy days;

Chapter Four – Rounding Out the Family. Again, completely True. This true story helps set-up the tale of the family and lets the reader know how nicely we *fitted-in* to the fabric of life in Medowie;

Chapter Five – Medowie Primary School. True, which just shows how small and quaint our little primary school was and how great the teachers were who worked there for many years;

Chapter Six – School Canteen. Again, all True. Every school deserved an opportunity for kids to enjoy the variety of foods offered by the canteen, even if only for once a month;

Chapter Seven – My First Kiss. True, although much of the tale was embellished. Narelle did kiss me, and I did over-react a bit, but certainly not to the extent I've suggested above;

Chapter Eight – School Bee Hives. False. What kid, no matter how deranged, would do that to another kid who was highly allergic to bees. I do recall some of the kids talking about doing something like this for a laugh, but it was never seriously considered and it certainly never happened;

Chapter Nine – Sticks Up Skirts. False, again, to a point. Sticks Up Skirts was suggested at some stage in maybe third class, and we did experiment playing a simple version of the game at recess a few times but once the teachers saw what was about to eventuate, they made sure the game never really "took off";

Chapter Ten – School Fete and Pet Competition. True and False. We had a School Fete annually, which was a lot of fun and enjoyed by all. There also was a Pet Show, but only once that I can recall. I did walk our cow around to the school for that show, and it did take hours both there and back. There was no competition with prizes and certificates, however, and there was definitely no *"Barry the Budgerigar"*;

Chapter Eleven – Family Life in Medowie. True. Country life for the kids of Medowie really was great fun and I'm sure this would be true across many country towns and regions in Australia. We all enjoyed the bush and the episodes of mischief which came with growing up. I'm also sure we pushed the boundaries a bit, but generally most of the kids were just good kids having a bit of fun;

Chapter Twelve – The Chook House. True. Jude and I did push Diane off the "chook house" roof and she did crawl up the driveway for help. We laughed a lot during that fun afternoon. I also cut my foot open on a rusted-out corrugated iron tank, and bled throughout the house, but there was no long-term damage done;

Chapter Thirteen – Little Kid Syndrome. True. I was given an axe to play with when I was about three years old, and I did cut Dad's extension cord into small pieces. There were also plenty of fires lit by many people around the Medowie bushland areas, some accidental and some on purpose;

Chapter Fourteen – Rusty the Wonder Dog. Sadly false. I did not have a dog called Rusty, in fact I never had a dog of my own. The family had a dog called "Buster" when I was very young, and I believe he was run over by a car, so no, not true;

Chapter Fifteen – Time to Get Back to Work. True. Mum needed to go back to work as the family needed the money. We did enjoy all of the social benefits of the RAAF Base back in the day, and it was genuinely a lot of fun growing up so close to this Defence Base;

Chapter Sixteen – Over-Active Imaginations. All these stories are True. My siblings and I did "make much mischief" as described and we often felt the full wrath of our parents. Before Mum and Dad moved house (after living on acres for many years), Dad did cut up the billiard table with an axe and throw it away. Sad, but true;

Chapter Seventeen – Punishment. Mostly True. Mum's punishment regime was exactly as suggested after any "indiscretion". She would make us line-up (from oldest to youngest) and walk down the line whacking us one at a time, until the "guilty party" confessed. It was often Diane, even though she was never guilty. I did bury many of Mum's preferred "weapons" in the yard, just for fun, of course;

Chapter Eighteen – The Big Linen Cupboard. True. It would be fair to say, however, that I've completely embellished the story, but the basic premise is true. I can't remember lying in wait for seven hours, but it was quite a long time, and I did scare the "living daylights" out of Mum when she opened the linen cupboard door;

Chapter Nineteen – Religion / Sunday School. False. I didn't steal money from the plate at Church, although I do recall thinking how easy it would be to do, which is exactly how I've described in the chapter. I feel guilty, just the same, for even thinking about doing it;

Chapter Twenty – The Broken Lounge. True. I broke the back leg off Mum and Dad's new expensive lounge, and I did get into a significant amount of trouble. None of my siblings would even entertain owning up to this one. They immediately pointed the finger at me and said in unison "... *it was Michael* ..." Understandably so;

Chapter Twenty-One – My 10th Birthday. Absolute rubbish. I made the whole episode up about my 10th birthday, however I have retold the story many times over the years, purely because I enjoy it so much. Many people have believed the story, and have expressed a "tinge" of sadness about my sad, lonely childhood. That is, of course, until they find out the whole story is just a lie;

Chapter Twenty-Two – Bushmaster's Craft Lessons. False. There was no such thing as "Bushmasters Craft Lessons" groups, that I'm aware of, when I was growing up and there certainly were none in operation around Medowie. I must admit I have always thought the tale to be funny, so I have retold it a few times over the years, despite it being a complete lie;

Chapter Twenty-Three – The Freedom of the Open Road. True. The pushbike ride home from primary school happened exactly as described. It did hurt a lot, and my bike was significantly damaged. Dad did spend much of his time repairing my bike afterwards for which I was eternally grateful;

Chapter Twenty-Four – Christmas in Medowie. Mostly True. Christmas was such a special time for us all growing up, and we did get to enjoy a real tree which we had sourced and cut down from the surrounding bushland. All of the families in Medowie would have sourced Christmas Tree in a similar fashion and it was genuinely a great time of the year. I did light a huge fire out the back to get rid of the wrapping paper and cardboard after we had opened our presents, but I've exaggerated a tad when I say I nearly burnt the house down;

Chapter Twenty-Five – Happy New Year. True. Exactly as told, too. Raymond and I love retelling the story of the day Pop got a fish-bone stuck in his arse: just gold. Really, Nan did deserve a medal for her performance in removing the fishbone but the less you think about that the better, I think;

Chapter Twenty-Six – Family Holidays. True. We did enjoy a holiday as a family, generally about once a year, where possible, and yes, I did bury my brand-new watch in the sand. Oh, the shame of it all;

Chapter Twenty-Seven – School Christmas Play and Presentation. Mostly True. The School Play was accurate to the point I was like the director and Jeffrey didn't turn up, so I filled in for him. I did come second in the Public Speaking, and Valerie did win, but the story itself is way out of perspective. Exaggerated almost to the point of disbelief I would say;

Chapter Twenty-Eight – The End of Primary School. True. We were off to High School the next year, and the teachers were excited for us. They answered our questions and told to try and relax because, whilst it was all new to us, we would work out it quickly and learn to cope. The sandpit episode with Christine was also true, which is funny now but a tad embarrassing at the time;

Chapter Twenty-Nine – Love Struck. True but, again, embellished. I didn't soil my trousers, but the story does demonstrate the feelings of a younger sibling when he has older sisters, and how invisible you can feel around their friends. So rather than being an embarrassment I think I was just "hanging around" for no real reason. My sisters would often say "… we don't know who he is …" or, for the friends of theirs who knew me, they would just say "… don't go near him – he's a sociopath …" High praise indeed.

And so, the tale of my younger years comes to an end.

Not sure how many readers guessed all of the lies, and each of the true stories, but certainly a bit of fun was had by all of my siblings (and me of course) during our formative years. Mum and Dad, on the other hand, could have "killed us" at times when we were growing up, but they did enjoy the retelling of these tales over the latter years of their lives. They certainly did a great job in raising five kids, too, so everyone was a winner, I guess.

Time seems to heal all, as they say in the classics.

The End